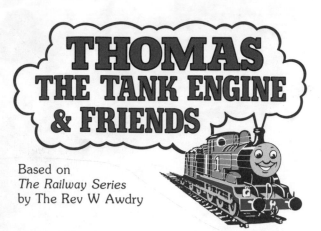

THOMAS
THE TANK ENGINE
& FRIENDS

Based on
The Railway Series
by The Rev W Awdry

Ladybird Books

Acknowledgment
*Photographic stills by Kenny McArthur of Clearwater Features
for Britt Allcroft (Thomas) Ltd.*

British Library Cataloguing in Publication Data
Awdry, W.
    Edward, Gordon and Henry; Gordon off the rails.—
    (Thomas the tank engine & friends; 6)
    I. Title   II. Awdry, W. Gordon off the rails
    III. Series
    823′.914[J]   PZ7
    ISBN 0-7214-0908-3

EDWARD, GORDON & HENRY

Edward, Gordon and Henry

Gordon, the big engine, always pulls the express. He is very proud of being the only engine strong enough to do so.

One day Gordon left the station with the express as usual. It was full of

important people, like the Fat Controller, and Gordon was seeing just how fast he could go.

"Hurry! Hurry!" he said.

"Trickety-trock, trickety-trock, trickety-trock," said the coaches.

Gordon went very fast and soon he could see the tunnel where Henry stood, bricked up and lonely.

Henry had been very foolish. He had gone into the tunnel and wouldn't come out again because he was afraid that the rain would spoil his lovely green paint.

The guard had blown his whistle; the fireman and passengers had argued with him; the men had pulled and pushed him but still Henry would not move.

Then, at last, they had given up. The
Fat Controller had ordered the men to
take up the old rails and to build a wall in
front of Henry. The other engines had to
use the tunnel at the other side.

Now Henry wondered if he would ever pull trains again.

"Oh dear! Will the Fat Controller ever forgive me and let me out?" he said to himself that day, as he watched Gordon getting closer and closer to the tunnel.

"In a minute," Gordon said, "I'm going to poop-poop at Henry and rush through the tunnel and out again into the open!"

He was almost there when, crack, "WHEEE————EESHSHSH!"

"You've burst a safety valve," said the driver. "You can't pull the train any more."

"Oh dear," said Gordon. "We were going so nicely, too. And look, there's Henry laughing at me!"

All the passengers climbed out of the coaches and came to see Gordon.

"Humph!" said the Fat Controller. "I never liked these big engines — always going wrong. Send for another engine at once."

They uncoupled Gordon. He had just enough puff to slink slowly into the siding, out of the way.

The guard went back to the yard to fetch another engine.

There was only Edward left in the shed.

"Gordon has burst a safety valve. Can you help?" asked the guard.

"I'll come and try," said Edward.

When Edward and the guard arrived back at the tunnel, Gordon was very rude. "Pooh!" he said. "Edward can't pull the train."

But they took no notice and Edward was coupled up behind the express. Edward puffed and pushed and pushed and puffed, but he couldn't move the heavy coaches.

"I told you so," said Gordon, rudely. "Why not let Henry try?"

"Yes, I will," said the Fat Controller.

"Henry, will you help to pull this train?" he asked.

"Oh yes!" said Henry, at once. "At last," he said to himself, "the Fat Controller *has* forgiven me."

So Gordon's driver and fireman lit Henry's fire. They broke down the wall and put back the rails. When Henry had built up steam, he puffed backwards out of the tunnel.

He was dirty and his boiler was black. He was covered in cobwebs. "Ooh! I'm so stiff. I'm so stiff," he groaned.

"Have a run to ease your joints and then find a turntable," said the Fat Controller, kindly.

When Henry came back he felt much better. Then they coupled him up at the front of Gordon's coaches.

"Peep, peep!" said Edward. "I'm ready!"

"Peep, peep, peep!" said Henry. "So am I!"

They started off. "Pull hard. We'll do it. Push hard. We'll do it," they puffed together.

Slowly the heavy coaches jerked and
began to move. Then off they went,
leaving Gordon alone in the siding. They
went faster and faster. "We've done it
together! We've done it together!" said
Edward and Henry.

"You've done it, hurray! You've done
it, hurray!" sang the coaches.

All the passengers were excited. The Fat Controller leaned out of the window to wave to Henry and Edward. But the train was going so fast that his hat blew off into a field where a goat ate it for tea!

The engines didn't stop until they came to the station at the end of the line. All the passengers climbed out and thanked Henry and Edward.

The Fat Controller was very pleased. He promised Henry a new coat of paint.

On their way home, Edward and Henry helped Gordon back to the shed.

All three engines are now great friends. Henry doesn't mind the rain any more. He knows that the best way to keep his paint looking nice is not to run into tunnels but to ask his driver to rub him down when the day's work is over.

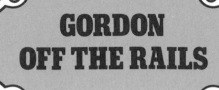

GORDON
OFF THE RAILS

Gordon off the rails

Gordon was resting in a siding. Sometimes, when he was resting, he would say to himself, "It's really *very* tiring to be such a large and splendid engine. One does have to keep up appearances so."

At that moment Henry came by. "Peep, peep! Peep, peep! Hello, Fatface!" whistled Henry. Gordon had not seen Henry for some time.

"What a cheek!" he spluttered. "That Henry is getting too big for his wheels. Fancy speaking to me like that! *Meeee!*" he went on, letting off steam. "*Meee* who has never had an accident!"

Percy heard Gordon's last remark and he knew that it wasn't true.

"Aren't burst safety valves accidents?" Percy asked, innocently.

Gordon was very cross. He didn't like being teased and he knew that Percy was talking about the time when he, Gordon, had pulled the express too fast and had burst a safety valve.

"No indeed! High spirits! Might happen to any engine!" replied Gordon, huffily. "But, to come off the rails like Henry did when he was pulling *The Flying Kipper*...well, I ask you!" he went on. "Is it right? Is it decent?"

A few days later it was Henry's turn to take the express. Gordon watched him getting ready.

"Be careful, Henry," he said. "You're

not pulling *The Flying Kipper* now! Mind
you keep on the rails today!"

Henry snorted away. Gordon yawned
and went to sleep.

But he didn't sleep for very long.

"Wake up, Gordon!" said his driver. "A special train is coming in and we're to pull it."

"Is it coaches or trucks?" asked Gordon, sleepily.

"Trucks," said his driver.

"Trucks!" said Gordon, crossly. "Pah!"

The men lit Gordon's fire and oiled him ready for the run.

He needed to go on the turntable first so that he would be facing the right way.

His fire was slow to start and wouldn't burn.

They couldn't wait so Edward was called to help Gordon to the turntable.

"I won't go. I won't go," grumbled Gordon.

"Don't be silly. Don't be silly," puffed Edward.

At last Gordon was on the turntable. Edward was uncoupled and he backed away.

Gordon's driver and fireman jumped down to turn him round.

The movement had shaken Gordon's fire so that it was soon burning nicely.

Gordon was cross and he didn't care what he did. He waited until the table was halfway round and then his chance came. "I'll show them! I'll show them!" he hissed.

He moved slowly forward. He only meant to go a little way – just far enough to 'jam' the turntable and stop it turning.

But his plan was going wrong – he couldn't stop himself...

He slithered and slipped off the rails, down the embankment and settled in a ditch.

"OOOOOsh!" he hissed. "Get me out! Get me out!" he called.

His driver and fireman came to see him. "Not a hope," said his driver. "You're stuck, you silly great engine, don't you understand that?"

They telephoned the Fat Controller.
He could see Gordon from his window.
"So, Gordon didn't want to take the
special train of trucks and ran into a
ditch?" he answered from his office.

"What's that you say?" he went on.
"The special's waiting – well, tell Edward
to take it, please. And Gordon? Oh,
leave him where he is. We haven't time
to bother with him now!"

So there was Gordon, stuck in the ditch. Over on the other side, some little boys were chattering. "Coo!" they called. "Doesn't he look silly! They'll never get him out."

Then the boys began to sing:
Silly old Gordon fell in a ditch,
fell in a ditch,
fell in a ditch.
Silly old Gordon fell in a ditch,
all on a Monday morning!

Gordon lay in the ditch all day.
"Oh dear!" he thought. "I shall never get out."

But that evening the men brought floodlights. They used powerful jacks to lift Gordon and made a road of sleepers under his wheels to keep him out of the mud.

Strong wire ropes were fastened to his back end and James and Henry, pulling hard, at last managed to bring Gordon back to the rails.

Late that night Gordon crawled home, a sadder and wiser engine.